This book is a gift of

THE MORAGA WOMEN'S SOCIETY

Moraga Branch, Contra Costa County Library

Keeper for the Sea

KIMBERLEY SMITH BRADY / illustrated by PETER M. FIORE

SIMON & SCHUSTER

BOOKS FOR YOUNG READERS

SIMON & SCHUSTER BOOKS FOR YOUNG READERS
An imprint of Simon & Schuster Children's Publishing Division
1230 Avenue of the Americas, New York, New York 10020

SIMON & SCHUSTER BOOKS FOR YOUNG READERS is a trademark of Simon & Schuster.
Book design by Heather Wood
The text for this book is set in Aldus. The illustrations are rendered in oils.
Printed and bound in the United States of America
First Edition
2 4 6 8 10 9 7 5 3 1

Library of Congress Cataloging-in-Publication Data
Brady, Kimberley Smith.
Keeper for the sea / by Kimberley Smith Brady.
p.   cm.
Summary : In September a young girl and her grandfather go fishing for bluefish.
ISBN 0-689-80472-5
[1. Fishing—Fiction. 2. Grandfathers—Fiction.] I. Title.
PZ7.B72935Ke   1996   [E]—dc20   94-18506

For Keepers Shawn and Todd
Love, Mom

For my dad and my Lisa
P. M. F.

I N THE QUIET OF THE NIGHT,
beneath my September blanket, I am already dressed
when Grandpa whispers just to me, "Let's go."
Long warm pants and a flannel shirt promise to
keep me warm from dizzy offshore winds. Without
one peep I lace my shoes and tie my hood.

"Good fishermen are soundless," Grandpa
reminds me as we creep down the stairs on the
tips of our toes.

Still, the shiny wood beneath our hushed feet
squeaks after all and Grandpa winks. "We must
not wake the sleeping bluefish," he says. And I
remember even fishermen have rules.

At first the dark is too thick for me and I think about grabbing Grandpa's coat or leg or hand. Instead he holds my neck between his finger and his thumb and points me toward the sea. "Fishermen become braver as they wrinkle," he says.

Near the beginning of the beach where the earth softens into sand, we stop while Grandpa studies the sky. I peek, too, at the Little Dipper and wonder to myself what twinkling stars have to do with sleeping bluefish.

There are no clouds.
The moon is sliced.
And the night is barely breathing. But he
keeps watching way far out and I keep quietly
still.

"Yep," Grandpa finally speaks, and off we step to the place beside the ocean where some say the blues bite best.

Silently, more night fishermen rest along the jetty and wait with their poles, watching the sky like dogs watch cats and cats watch mice.

Grandpa and I move to the far end of the seawall where humps of saltwater break upon the rocks. *Swish. Swoosh.* The waves are politely hushed for the night breeze while she hums. *Swish. Swoosh. Hmm.* Back and forth. *Swish. Swoosh. Hmm.*

After Grandpa and I snap our fishing pole
together he shows me how to thread the line.
Then we wait.

I have heard tales of the fighting blues, how
they jig and spin and ride the tide, fiercely
snapping tested line. I have heard that their
razor-sharp teeth have gashed sea monsters
into bits and helpless jellyfish into smidgens.
But so far the night feels much too gentle for
a war of tugs.

Soon the sleepy night begins to stir, as softly swishing waves quicken to slams and the mumbled breeze shifts to a howl. Grandpa and all the other fishermen watch the waking sky. I look, too, as real fishermen do. *Kip-kip-kip*. At once, we all turn north to an easy flapping of wings and a far-off whine.

"See the terns shadowing the blues?" Grandpa asks. And against the sky I see zillions of white-bellied birds diving into the cold, hard water. Down and up, dashing back and forth, to and from their safe free flock.

"Terns feed on bunker herring the bluefish stir up," Grandpa tells me. "See the water boil?" I do see one patch of busy bubbles, in the middle of the silky sea, steering the terns our way. Closer and closer and closer.

"Ready?" Grandpa asks before casting his wily line into the ocean's simmering pot. Patiently, he smoothly rhythms cast and reel, cast and reel, over and over again, in and out of the bouncing waves.

Without one warning, the line zips tight
and bends the rod toward the sea.
  "Got one, Grandpa?" I ask.
  "Got one," he says.

In the beginning the fighting blue spins in big, wide circles. Grandpa lets it. When the fish finally tires, Grandpa wheels the handle on his reel around and around and around, nodding to me for help. Our hands circle up and down, dragging our bluefish closer to shore, one strong turn at a time.

The sun lifts just as our bucking blue breaks
through the water, twisting and jerking between
the ocean and the air. Blue silver scales leap
through the dawn, streaking the morning sky,
all the while kicking an angry white spray with
its reckless tail. From afar I see rows of terrible
teeth coming closer to shore, and to me.

On top of the seawall we reel and reel and reel until at last Grandpa hauls our catch upon the cold, gray stones. "Biggest blue I've ever seen," he puffs.

And all the curious fishermen along the ocean jetty come to say:

"Big blue."

"Great catch."

"Brought it in nice and slow."

Grandpa unhooks our fish and sinks down to
rest upon the wall. I rest, too, like weary fishermen
do. Our fish, with blue-gray scales and clear marble
eyes, squiggles toward the sea, thirsty for home.

"Grandpa, think it's a keeper?" I ask.
Smiling into the ocean, Grandpa answers
knowingly. "Fought too hard not to be." And
with sure hands he slides our bluefish back
beneath its seaweed blanket.

Now I know, too, what real fishermen do as
we walk home—to leave the night for the day,
the stars for the sun, the terns for the gulls.
And, a keeper for the sea.